O'Connor, Jane.
Eek! Stories to make you shriek / by Jane O'Connor ; illustrated by Brian Karas. -- New York : Grosset & Dunlap, c1992.

48 p. : ill. ; pc 2. -- (All aboard reading. Level 2.)

SUMMARY: Three easy-to-read scary stories about a talking doll, a dog picture that barks, and a Halloween monster.

ISBN 0-448-40383-8(lib.bdg.) : $7.99

1. Horror stories. 2. Short stories. I. Title. II. Series.

Put Beginning Readers on the Right Track with ALL ABOARD READING™

The All Aboard Reading series is especially for beginning readers. Written by noted authors and illustrated in full color, these are books that children really and truly *want* to read—books to excite their imagination, tickle their funny bone, expand their interests, and support their feelings. With three different reading levels, All Aboard Reading lets you choose which books are most appropriate for your children and their growing abilities.

Level 1—for Preschool through First Grade Children
Level 1 books have very few lines per page, very large type, easy words, lots of repetition, and pictures with visual "cues" to help children figure out the words on the page.

Level 2—for First Grade to Third Grade Children
Level 2 books are printed in slightly smaller type than Level 1 books. The stories are more complex but there is still lots of repetition in the text and many pictures. The sentences are quite simple and are broken up into short lines to make reading easier.

Level 3—for Second through Third Grade Children
Level 3 books have considerably longer texts, use harder words and more complicated sentences.

All Aboard for happy reading!

For Willie and Cornelia — J.O'C.

To John Wagner
for his help and friendship —B.K.

 Published by Grosset & Dunlap, Inc., which is a member of The Putnam & Grosset Group, New York. ALL ABOARD READING is a trademark of The Putnam & Grosset Group. Published simultaneously in Canada. Printed in the U.S.A.

Library of Congress Cataloging-in-Publication Data
O'Connor, Jane. Eek! Stories to make you shriek / by Jane O'Connor ; illustrated by Brian Karas. p. cm.—(All aboard reading) Summary: Three easy-to-read scary stories about a talking doll, a dog picture that barks, and a Halloween monster. 1. Horror tales, American. 2. Children's stories, American. [1. Horror stories. 2. Short stories.] I. Karas, Brian, ill. II. Title. III. Series. PZ7.0222Ee 1992 [E]—dc20 91-33674 CIP AC

ISBN 0-448-40383-8 (GB) A B C D E F G H I J
ISBN 0-448-40382-X (pbk.) A B C D E F G H I J

Level 2
Grades 1–3

EEK!

Stories to Make You Shriek

By Jane O'Connor
Illustrated by Brian Karas

Grosset & Dunlap • New York

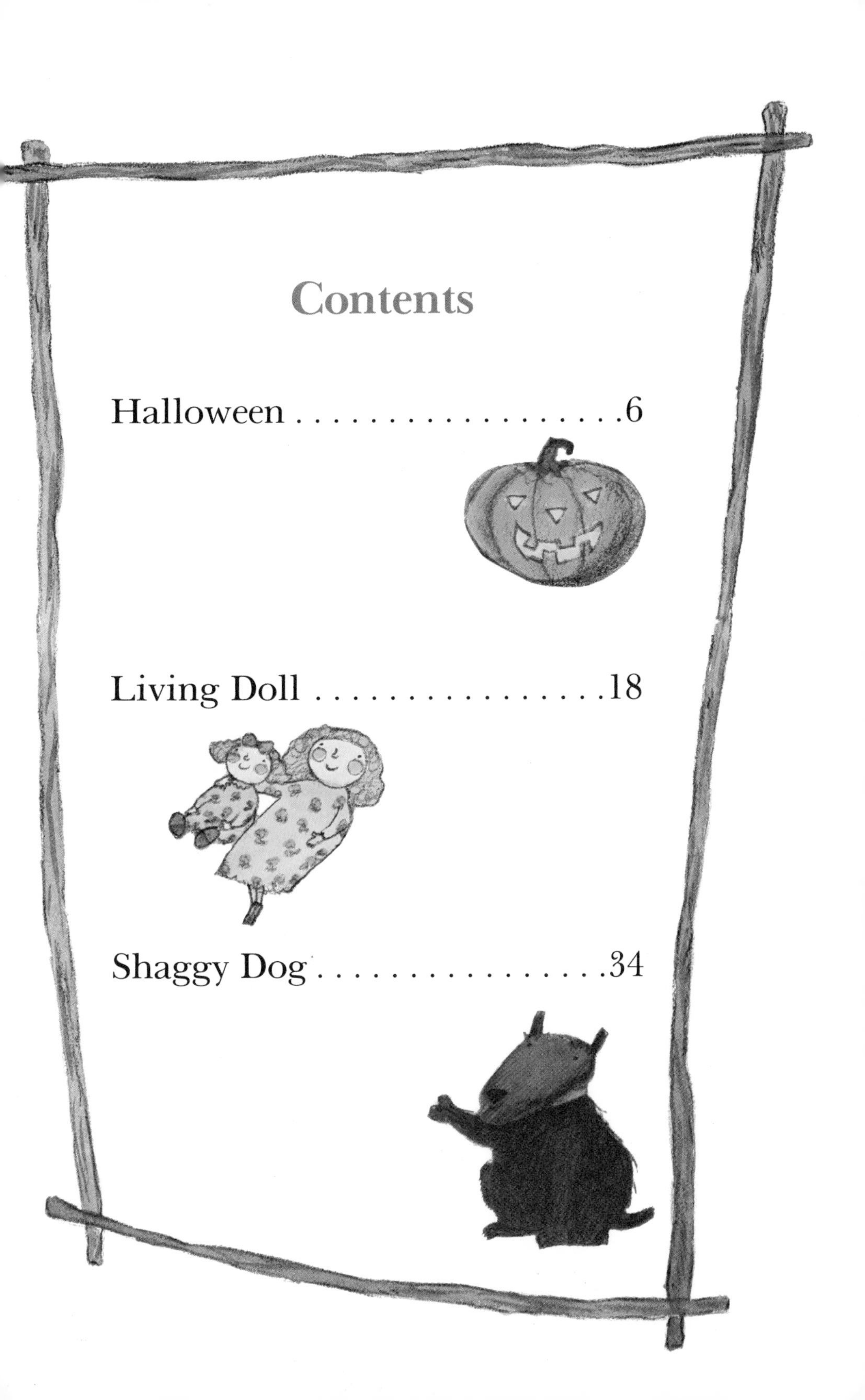

Contents

Halloween

It was Halloween.

Ted was waiting for his friend Danny.

They were going to a party.

Ted already had on his costume.

He wore white pants,

a white shirt,

a black belt,

and a black headband.

He was a karate guy.

"Be sure to wear a coat,"

Ted's mother called.

Ted made a face.

"Come on, Ma.

Karate guys do not wear coats."

Ted's mother did not care.

"It is cold out.

You wear a coat.

Or you cannot go to the party."

Ted made another face.

But he put on his coat.

Then he went to wait for Danny.

It was dark now.

The trees made spooky shadows

on the street.

Ted hoped Danny would come soon.

Then he saw Danny

coming down the street.

Danny was dressed as a monster.

He wore a furry brown suit

with furry paws and claws.

Over his head was a monster mask.

"Wow! Cool costume," said Ted.

"Gronk," was all Danny said.

Then off they went to the party.

The party was fun.

Everyone bobbed for apples

and ate pizza for dinner.

There was a costume contest.

Danny won.

"Gronk!" said Danny,

when he got the prize.

It was a big bag of candy.

On the way home

Danny ate all his candy.

He let out a big burp.

“Gross!” said Ted.

“Gronk!” said Danny.

Then Ted waved good-bye.

The next day Ted went to Danny's house.

They always walked to school together.

Danny's mother opened the door.

"Danny is sick," she said.

"He cannot go to school today."

Ted felt bad.

"I bet it was all the junk

Danny ate at the party," said Ted.

Danny's mother looked puzzled.

"The party?

Danny did not go to the party.

He was sick in bed all night,"

said Danny's mother.

Then <u>who</u> was the monster at the party?

Living Doll

Sara Beth always got her way.

If she wanted to stay up late,

her mother let her.

If she wanted to eat

nothing but ice cream,

her mother let her.

All Sara Beth had to say was,

"I want it."

And any toy was hers.

One day Sara Beth and her mother
passed a store.
In the window was a mama doll
and a baby doll.

The baby doll had yellow hair

and a pretty smile.

"I want her," said Sara Beth.

She pulled her mother into the store.

"How much is the baby doll?"

Sara Beth asked.

The lady smiled.

"The mama doll and the baby doll are a set.

They cost $50."

Sara Beth stamped her foot.

"I don't want the mama.

I only want the baby!"

Sara Beth's mother paid the lady.

"Here is all the money.

But we will just take the baby doll."

Sara Beth took her new doll home.

She took it out of the box.

Did her doll look different somehow?

No. Sara Beth's eyes were playing tricks on her.

Then Sara Beth put the doll

beside her bed.

That night Sara Beth woke up.

"MAMA!" someone was shouting.

It was her new doll!

The lady had not said

it was a talking doll.

Did the doll look mad?

Or was it in Sara Beth's mind?

Sara Beth was scared.

Sara Beth shouted for her mother
and dived under the covers.
"What's wrong, dear?"
her mother asked.
"My doll!
She was shouting at me.
And she looks mad,"
Sara Beth cried.

"She looks the same to me,"

said Sara Beth's mother.

Sara Beth took another look.

The doll was smiling.

Sara Beth shook it.

But the doll did not say "Mama."

It did not say anything at all.

"You must have been
having a bad dream,"
said her mother.
"Go back to sleep.
Your doll is fine."

MAMA!

MAMA

MAMA!

So Sara Beth went back to sleep.

But soon she woke up again.

Something was poking her.

It was the doll!

It was in Sara Beth's bed.

How did it get there?

"MAMA! I WANT MY MAMA!"

the doll shouted.

"TAKE ME BACK!"

Sara Beth nodded.

She was too scared to say a word.

MAMA!
MAMA!
MAMA!
MAMA!

The very next day
Sara Beth took the doll
back to the store.
The lady put the doll
in the window.
It was next
to the mama doll again.

Sara Beth looked back just once.

Yes.

The doll was smiling again.

Shaggy Dog

The Greens were moving

into their new house.

The house was big.

But the Greens were a big family.

Dad parked the van.

Right away

Mother made all the kids

take stuff inside.

"I do not like empty houses,"

Mother told everyone.

But the house was not empty.

As soon as the Greens opened the door,

a dog ran up to them.

A big, black shaggy dog.

"WOOF!" the dog barked.

Then he held out his paw.

The Greens all laughed.

"Oh boy!" shouted the kids.

"A dog came with the house!

Can we keep him?"

Dad shook his head.

"No. This dog belongs to someone.

Don't you, big guy?"

The dog barked again.
Then he trotted over
to a picture on the wall.
"He wants to tell us something,"
Mother said.

The picture was of a boy and a dog.

The boy had thrown a stick in the air.

The dog was jumping to catch it.

What was the shaggy dog trying to say?

Was he lost?

Did he belong to the family

who used to live in the house?

Was the picture theirs too?

The Greens did not know.

Dad took both the dog
and the picture out to the garage.
He made a bed for the dog.
"You will stay here for the night.
And tomorrow we will find out
who you belong to."

Later that night there was a storm.

The shaggy dog ran to the back door.

"Woof! Woof! Woof!" he barked.

"Oh, no! You cannot come in,"

Mother said.

"You are much too muddy.

I am taking you back to the garage."

And that is what she did.

By the next morning the storm was over.

"Why don't you give the dog
a bath in the yard?"
Mother said to the children.
"Then we can take him
over to the police station."
But when the children went
to the garage,
they did not see the dog.

How did he get out?

The door had been closed.

The children ran to the yard.

"Here, boy!" they called.

But the dog did not come.

Was he down the street?

No!

Had he sneaked into the house?

No!

Then they heard barking.

Loud barking.

It was coming from the garage!

The children ran in and shouted,

"You were here all along!"

But they were wrong.

There was no dog—

only some boxes and

the old picture from the house.

The children stood as still as statues.

They could not believe their eyes.

Now two dogs were in the picture.

They were both jumping for the stick.

The new dog was big and black and shaggy.

What had happened?

The Greens never knew.

But they never saw

the big shaggy dog again.